**Austin Flint**

# Manual of Chemical Examination of the Urine in Disease

Anatiposi

Austin Flint

# Manual of Chemical Examination of the Urine in Disease

Reprint of the original.

1st Edition 2023 | ISBN: 978-3-38211-146-5

Anatiposi Verlag is an imprint of Outlook Verlagsgesellschaft mbH.

Verlag (Publisher): Outlook Verlag GmbH, Zeilweg 44, 60439 Frankfurt, Deutschland
Vertretungsberechtigt (Authorized to represent): E. Roepke, Zeilweg 44, 60439 Frankfurt, Deutschland
Druck (Print): Books on Demand GmbH, In de Tarpen 42, 22848 Norderstedt, Deutschland

# MANUAL

OF

## CHEMICAL EXAMINATION

OF THE

# URINE IN DISEASE;

WITH

BRIEF DIRECTIONS FOR THE EXAMINATION OF THE MOST
COMMON VARIETIES OF URINARY CALCULI.

BY

## AUSTIN FLINT, Jr. M. D

PROFESSOR OF PHYSIOLOGY AND MICROSCOPY IN THE BELLEVUE HOSPITAL
MEDICAL COLLEGE, NEW YORK; FELLOW OF THE NEW YORK ACADEMY
OF MEDICINE; MEMBER OF THE MEDICAL SOCIETY OF THE
COUNTY OF NEW YORK; RESIDENT MEMBER OF THE
LYCEUM OF NATURAL HISTORY IN THE CITY
OF NEW YORK, ETC., ETC.

*SECOND EDITION, REVISED AND CORRECTE.*

NEW YORK:
D. APPLETON AND COMPANY,
549 & 551 BROADWAY.
1871.

# PREFACE TO THE SECOND EDITION.

THE demand for a second edition, so soon after the first issue of this little work, has afforded me an early opportunity for correcting several important errors in some of the tables copied from English authors. These corrections have been made by Dr. Thomas Ryerson, of Newton, N. J., who has carefully revised all of my tables and formulæ. The error into which I fell, in copying table C from Golding Bird, is due to the difference between the imperial fluidounce, of 455·69 grains, used in Great Britain, and the apothecaries' fluidounce, of 437·5 grains, used in this country. In the new table the reduction has been carefully made to wine-measure, and the table has been extended to from 1001 to 1042, inclusive. A corresponding error occurs in the translation of Fehling's formula, taken from

Roberts, which is also erroneous in the proportion of the soda solution, estimated by volume in the translation, while it is taken by weight in the original.

NEW YORK, 125 EAST THIRTY-SIXTH STREET,
*July* 1, 1870.

# PREFACE TO THE FIRST EDITION.

SEVERAL months ago, I suggested to Messrs. Tiemann & Co., of this city, the desirability of arranging a set of tests, etc., for such urinary examinations as are now constantly required by the medical practitioner; and I proposed to supervise the work and write a few simple directions for use, to accompany the apparatus; but as I progressed, it became evident that the directions, to be complete and satisfactory, should be much more extended than I at first supposed, and they finally assumed the dimensions of this little volume.

Microscopical examinations of the urinary deposits form, often, an indispensable element in diagnosis and prognosis; but, much more frequently, a very simple chemical examination of the urine, such as can and should be made by the physician,

will answer all practical purposes. I concluded, for
the present at least, not to touch upon urinary deposits, a subject which can only be adequately considered in extended treatises, but to confine myself
to the chemical study of the urine in disease, with
very brief directions for the examination of the
most common forms of urinary calculi; and I have
prefaced these practical points with a few introduc-
tory remarks concerning the variations in the properties and composition of the urine under normal
conditions.

My chief aim, in the preparation of this little
work, has been to enable the busy practitioner to
make for himself, rapidly and easily, all ordinary
examinations of urine, and to give him the benefit
of my own experience in eliminating little difficulties in the manipulations, and in reducing processes
of analysis to the utmost simplicity that is consistent with accuracy. Having for many years been
daily in the habit of making chemical and microscopical examinations of the urine for physicians, I
felt that I was able to appreciate pretty thoroughly
what is required in ordinary practice.

My first object was to arrange a standard set of apparatus, simple, yet sufficient for all practical purposes. I have spared no time or pains in my endeavors to accomplish this end; and the makers have pledged themselves not to dispose of the set or any part of the set, which I have thoroughly tested, and which is to remain in their possession as a standard of accuracy.

My next object was to remove as far as possible all of the difficulties which I had myself experienced in urinary examinations. I am fully aware of the fact that the processes suggested for the quantitative determination of the urea, chlorine, and sulphuric acid in the urine, are not absolutely accurate; but I have no hesitation in recommending them as sufficiently exact to meet all the requirements of the practical physician, while their simplicity and the facility of their application put them within the reach of every one.

I had hoped to be able to apply the volumetric method, which has proved so convenient in such analyses, to all of the examinations of the urine that are now recognized as important to the physician;

but after a patient trial of the volumetric analysis
for uric acid by a graduated solution of the per-
manganate of potassa, I have become convinced
that this process is so wanting in accuracy as to be
unavailable, even for rough estimates. I am indebted to my assistant, Mr. J. W. S. Arnold, for a
simplification of the process for quantitative analysis for this principle, which is sufficiently easy,
though it occupies some time and requires the use
of a tolerably delicate balance. There is at present
no volumetric process for estimating uric acid, that
is at all reliable.

I have taken great care in the preparation of
some new tables, by which the necessary calculations are so simplified that the quantities of most
of the important normal and abnormal ingredients
of the urine may be ascertained almost instantly.
I have also given a full table of the normal variations in the properties and composition of
the urine. These tables are all printed upon a
single sheet at the end of the volume; and, if
this be cut out and posted in a conspicuous place
for reference, after a little practice it will be seldom

necessary to consult the book itself in the progress of an examination.

If these objects be but in part accomplished, and if the attention of physicians can be directed more frequently to the condition of the urine in disease, this little book, with its modest pretensions and imperfect execution, will not be without value to the profession.

New York, 125 East Thirty-sixth Street,
*January* 1. 1870.

# CONTENTS.

## INTRODUCTION.

## CHAPTER I.

### QUALITATIVE EXAMINATIONS OF THE URINE.

## CHAPTER II.

### QUANTITATIVE ANALYSIS OF THE URINE.

# APPENDIX.

URINARY CALCULI AND GRAVEL—CARE OF APPARATUS.

## TABLES.

---

## LIST OF ILLUSTRATIONS.

# CHEMICAL EXAMINATION

OF THE

# URINE IN DISEASE.

---

## INTRODUCTION.

Recognition of abnormal matters in the urine—Mode of production of excrementitious principles in the system—Mode of elimination of excrementitious principles by the kidneys—Variations in the general and physical properties of the normal urine—Normal variations in the elimination of urea and uric acid—Normal variations in the proportions of the inorganic constituents of the urine.

THE importance of urinary examinations, in their bearing upon diagnosis, treatment, and prognosis in disease, is now admitted by all who have kept pace with the progress of medical science during the last twenty-five or thirty years. Even if we except the examinations for sugar and for albumen, there are many conditions of the urine, involving either a modification in the proportion of its normal constituents or the presence of abnormal principles, which it is very important to recognize.

With regard to certain abnormal principles that may exist in the urine, it is essential to the practical physician, not only to be able to recognize their presence by simple and reliable tests, but, in many instances, to estimate their quantity. In diabetes mellitus, a knowledge of the fact that sugar exists in the urine is a necessary element in the diagnosis; and the influence of dietetic and other measures of treatment, in most cases, is speedily and certainly indicated by the modifications in the proportion of sugar in the urine. Indeed, it is impossible to treat this affection intelligently without estimating from time to time the quantity of sugar discharged by the kidneys. Albuminuria, which is so prominent a symptom in certain diseases of the kidneys that it is often spoken of as if it were in itself a disease, is a condition which must be recognized in the diagnosis of these disorders. It frequently happens that the presence of albumen in the urine is the first positive indication of a pathological condition of the kidneys, and this single fact directs the attention of the physician to an entire class of important diseases.

Physiologists are constantly progressing in the knowledge of the phenomena that attend the general process of nutrition of the organism, and, with every development in this direction, additional importance is attached to the examination of the urine in disease. The relations of physiology and pathology, as regards excretion, are to a considerable extent reciprocal. Pathologists cannot comprehend morbid changes in the process of disassimilation without a knowledge of the physiological conditions; and, on the other hand, modifications of the function of excretion in disease frequently aid the physiologist in determining the relations of certain excrementitious principles to the healthy organism.

There are few facts in physiology better established than that certain principles discharged from the body, called excrementitious, represent the physiological wear of the organism; and there is no avenue of discharge by which these effete matters are so uniformly excreted as by the urinary apparatus. The fæces contain the *débris* of food in addition to the certain peculiar excrementitious principles; the skin discharges its excretions in such a form that they are with difficulty collected and studied; but the urine is the type of the excretions; its composition is constantly varying in health, and is almost of necessity modified in disease; and this fluid may be collected and analyzed so easily, that, certainly, the clinical student should only be restricted in the practical applications of the changes in this fluid in disease by the limits of physiological knowledge of the relations of the different excrementitious principles to the organism.

It may be useful, as an introduction to the clinical study of the urine, to sketch briefly the mode of production of certain of its constituents, and their elimination by the kidneys. There is every reason to believe that all excrementitious matters are produced in the general system, are taken up by the blood in circulating through the tissues, and are separated from the blood and thrown off by the proper organs. The kidneys have nothing to do with the formation of the urinary principles; they simply purify the blood by separating from it certain effete matters. Supposing, then, that the kidneys be perfectly healthy, serious modifications in the urinary excretion may occur, depending upon diseases in the general system. It is not disease of the kidneys that gives rise to the presence of sugar in the urine, or to an excess of urea, urates, uric acid, phosphates, etc.; but these changes are due to disturbances in nutrition and disassimilation. An excessive production of uric acid in the system may give rise to calculus, to certain general symptoms, and yet the kidneys be perfectly normal; and such examples as this might be multiplied. On the other hand, the general nutritive processes may be normal, except as they are secondarily influenced through the kidneys, and very grave disorders of the urinary excretion may be due exclusively to structural disease of the kidneys themselves, by which they are rendered incapable of separating the required quantity of excrementitious matter from the blood.

The distinction between the two conditions just mentioned should be kept constantly in view in practice. In the great majority of instances, though not invariably, if there be serious structural disease of the kidneys, there will be albumen in the urine. The physician should fully appreciate the importance of this symptom, albuminuria, as pointing to disease of the kidneys, it may be, of a transient character, or it may be in the form of an irremediable structural lesion. Having the attention thus directed to the kidneys, it becomes an important question to decide how far these organs are capable of performing their function; and, in the great majority of cases, the efficiency of their action may be measured by the daily discharge of urea, the most important of the solid constituents of the urine. I mention urea as the principle to be watched in these cases, because it is formed by the system in greater quantity, and accumulates in the blood, when its elimination by the kidneys is interrupted, more rapidly than any other of the urinary constituents.

If it be impossible to determine the existence of structural disease of the kidneys by the presence of albumen in the urine or by microscopical examination of the urinary sediment, it is generally, if not always, fair to assume that any changes in the composition in the urine, beyond its ordinary physiological variations, are due to conditions of nutrition involving the original production of the excrementitious principles in the general system. These conditions may affect the quantity of the urine, its color, odor, specific gravity, or reaction, and may modify the proportion of urea, of urates, chlorides, sulphates, phosphates, and perhaps other of its constituents, the physiological relations of which are as yet imperfectly understood.

It is not contemplated, in this little work, to discuss the significance of all the variations from the healthy standard, but, in the study of the urine in disease, it is absolutely necessary to keep in view the purely physiological conditions capable of modifying this excretion.

Physiologically, the variations in the quantity, color, and specific gravity of the urine bear a certain relation to each other. When the skin is acting very freely, and when the solid elements are increased by exercise, the quantity of urine is apt to tend toward the minimum, the specific gravity being high and the color, though normal in character, of a deeper shade. This is most likely to occur when liquids are ingested in small quantity. On the other hand, when the skin is not active, as in very cold weather, the urine will probably approach the maximum in quantity, the specific gravity being low and the color light. The ingestion of large quantities of liquid will often induce, as a temporary condition, an abundant secretion of fluid of low density. In these conditions the real amount of solid excretion is not much affected, the difference being simply in the dilution of the urine. When the density is very low and the secretion scanty, showing an evident deficiency in the activity of the kidneys, one is led to look for evidences of disease of these organs, the most prominent indication of which is albuminuria. When the specific gravity is very high and the quantity normal or increased, there may be reason to suspect the presence of some abnormal solid matter in solution in the urine, and the principle most likely to be present is sugar. The normal conditions above enumerated, are, however, capable of temporarily affecting the specific gravity to such an extent, that a specimen may present as low a density as 1005 or higher than 1030,

without being, in itself, positive evidence of disease.

The odor of the urine varies, in the intensity
of its "urinous" character, with the proportion of
solid matter.   Some albuminous urine of very low
density is almost inodorous.   Saccharine urine is
apt to have a sweetish odor.   Some phosphatic
urine has an excessively fetid odor.   It must be
remembered, also, that peculiar odorous principles
are sometimes developed in the urine after taking
certain remedies, as turpentine, or particular articles of food, as asparagus.   In clinical examinations it is frequently quite important to take ac-
count of the odor of the urine in connection with
the more elaborate processes of analysis.

The reaction of the urine varies, in health, with
digestion and other circumstances.   Vegetable food
diminishes the acidity and may render the urine
alkaline, while animal food has the opposite effect.
The rapid development of a free acid in the urine
after it has been passed, may of itself decompose
the urates, and be the sole cause of the deposition
of uric acid; and a deposit of the triple phosphates
may, on the other hand, be due entirely to an alkaline condition of the urine.   It is sometimes an important element in the treatment of disease to keep
the urine alkaline, so that it is frequently very

desirable to take note of the reaction, as well as of the other general properties of the urine.

In estimating the urea in the urine, which is so often required in practice, it is a point of the greatest importance to keep in view the physiological variations in the proportion of this principle. Before the age of fifteen or eighteen years, the amount of urea and other solid matters excreted by the kidneys, in proportion to the weight of the body, is much greater than in the adult. In women the normal excretion of urea is generally less than in men; and when the amount of food taken is habitually small and the muscular system is very inactive, the amount of urea may be very much diminished from these causes alone. In persons confined to the bed with any disease, and taking but little food, the urea may be small in quantity without indicating disease of the kidneys. Exercise increases the production of urea, and animal food has the same influence to a marked degree. It has been ascertained that a purely animal diet will increase the amount of urea fully two-fifths; a vegetable diet will diminish it one-third; and a nonnitrogenized diet will reduce it more than one-half. It can be readily understood that these facts become exceedingly important in estimating the urea discharged in disease. In what is known as Bright's disease, it very often happens that the condition of the general nutrition of the body becomes such as to lead to a very great diminution in the actual production of urea, and the quantity in the urine may be small, and yet the kidneys be separating from the blood all that is formed in the system.

Inasmuch as the production of urea is profoundly affected by the quality of food, and as one of the great dangers to be feared in serious structural disease of the kidneys is uræmia, it would seem as important to diminish the production of urea by a change in diet, as to adopt measures to favor its elimination from the system. It is certainly a reasonable supposition that the danger from uræmia would be diminished, if the production of urea be reduced by regulating the ingesta, particularly with reference to nitrogenized matters.

Nearly the same remarks that have been made concerning the production of urea are applicable to uric acid. This principle always exists in health in the form of urates, the proportion of which is exceedingly variable under normal conditions. The pathological relations of uric acid, particularly in gout and in diseases accompanied with urinary concretions, cannot be adequately discussed within the limits of this work.

In making quantitative examinations of the

urine for chlorides, sulphates, and phosphates, it must be remembered that the normal variations in these constituents are even greater than the fluctuations of urea and the urates, and that they are to a great extent dependent upon diet. It is not often, indeed, that much valuable information is to be derived from estimates of the proportions of the inorganic matters in the urine; still, there are certain pathological conditions in which the proportion of some of these principles is modified, particularly the chlorides, for a consideration of which the reader is referred to elaborate works on the urine. In this brief introduction, I designed only to mention some of the most important of the physiological variations in the properties and composition of the urine, as a necessary preparation to the study of this excretion in disease.

2

# CHAPTER I.

## QUALITATIVE EXAMINATIONS OF THE URINE.

Apparatus for urinary examinations—Method of obtaining a specimen for examination—General appearance, color, and odor of the urine—Reaction—Specific gravity—Presence or absence of albumen—Presence or absence of sugar—Presence or absence of bile.

IT is now so easy to make examinations of the urine extended and accurate enough for ordinary clinical purposes, that there is no good reason why physicians, especially recent graduates, should not be able to ascertain for themselves most of the important facts to be learned from a urinary analysis, and this without an undue expenditure of time and pains. A very simple examination, indeed, will suffice to exclude diseases of the kidneys and disorders of the general system that are attended with serious modifications in the composition of the urine; but it must frequently happen that a more extended analysis is required and should be made at once, and this many practitioners are not prepared to undertake.

Although many attempts have been made to devise a cheap, convenient, and sufficiently complete set of apparatus for ordinary examinations of the urine, few if any of them have been extensively used. It has seemed to me that this can be readily explained. A practitioner wants, in the first place, a convenient place and a quick and easy method for making his examinations, and his apparatus should be always ready for use; and none of the very cheap and compact sets of reagents will answer these requirements. An apparatus constructed on this principle is like a pocket microscope, convenient enough for transportation, but difficult and trying to the patience in actual use. A physician should be provided with a good, firm table, at least four feet by two, with drawers for stowing away odd articles, and a sufficiently complete chemical apparatus to enable him to do all his work conveniently. He should see that his apparatus is always clean and ready for use, and that his solutions are kept in order. The table should be in a good light, for microscopical as well as chemical work; and, in short, it should be so furnished that he is able to do his work with the least possible trouble. He should have, in conspicuous places, tables and formulæ for facilitating his calculations, and should be provided, in some way, with means of recording the most important of the results of his examinations. A compact and scanty set of apparatus is always inconvenient, is usually in disorder, and will not answer for constant use.

Having for some years been in the habit of making frequent examinations of the urine for physicians, I have been led to arrange a set of apparatus that I have found by experience to be the most convenient for daily use. I have not, however, been accustomed to subject the sediment to chemical tests, but have always used the microscope, as the simplest and most rapid method of ascertaining the character of urinary deposits. The microscopical characters of the urine in disease I shall not describe; for, although the application of the microscope in this way is not difficult, the subject of urinary deposits is too extended to be adequately considered within the limits of this work, and reliable treatises on the subject are sufficiently accessible. Among the best, is a recent work by Dr. Roberts, which has been republished in this country.[1]

The following solutions are sufficient for ordinary clinical examinations of the urine:

---

[1] ROBERTS, *A Practical Treatise on Urinary and Renal Diseases, including Urinary Deposits.* Philadelphia, 1866.

*List of Apparatus.*

Case of Reagents, containing—

1. Nitric acid.
2. Hydrochloric acid.
3. Acetic acid.
4. Nitroso-nitric acid.
5. Nitrate of silver in solution (9·58 grains in an ounce).
6. Sulphate of copper in solution (94·73 grains in an ounce).
7. Neutral tartrate of potash in solution (378·91 grains in an ounce).
8. Solution of soda (specific gravity 1·12).
9. Liquor potassæ.
10. Liquor ammoniæ.
11. Ether.
12. Mercury.
13. Solution of hypochlorite of soda.
14. Solution of chloride of sodium (saturated)
15. Test-paper.
16. German yeast.
    A. Urinometer.
    B. Thermometer.
    C. Graduated glasses.
        (*a.*) Six ounce.
        (*b.*) One ounce graduated in drachms.
        (*c.*) One drachm.

D. 4 conical glasses with porcelain covers.

E. Porcelain evaporating-dishes, and watch-glasses.

F. Test-tube stands with test-tubes.

G. 3 funnels and filtering-paper.

H. 3 flasks and wire gauze.

I. Bunsen's burner, rubber tubing, etc., or alcohol lamp.

K. Burette, graduated in grains.

L. 200 grain measure.

M. Tube graduated in cubic inches, with vessel in which it can be inverted.

N. Rings and clamp for graduated tube.

O. Stirring-rods and drop-tubes.

P. Swabs and brushes for cleaning.

R. Platinum spoon for calculi.

S. Blow-pipe.

T. Colored papers, gummed, for recording the color of specimens.


## Extra Apparatus.

A. Hydrometer of Baumé, for liquids heavier than water.

B. 1000 gr., 500 gr., and 100 gr. specific-gravity bottles.

E. 2 wash-bottles and 3 precipitating glasses.

F. A balance, at least delicate enough to turn with $\frac{1}{50}$ of a grain.

G. Graduated solution of chloride of barium, (36·6 grains in six fluidounces of water) for quantitative analysis for the sulphates.

H. Three separate solutions for quantitative analysis for phosphoric acid. 1. Sesqui-chloride of iron; 9·33 grains of iron by hydrogen dissolved in hydochloric with a little nitric acid, evaporated to dryness, and dissolved in six fluidounces of water. 2. 400 grains of acetate of soda and 800 grains of acetic acid dissolved in six fluidounces of water. 3. 12 grains of ferrocyanide of potassium dissolved in six fluidounces of water.

In ordinary examinations of the urine, a speci-men taken in the morning immediately after rising from bed will be found to represent, more nearly than any other, the general process of disassimilation. There are occasions in which it is desirable and indispensable to examine a specimen of the mixed urine of the twenty-four hours; but, in the great majority of cases, the morning urine will be sufficient, and this may be obtained without alarming the patient or friends, or leading them to suppose kidneys. I will therefore indicate, first, the process for an ordinary examination, by which it may be desired simply to exclude the question of urinary disturbance, and afterward describe more minutely the processes involved in more important investigations.

*Method of obtaining a Specimen for Examination.*—A specimen of the morning urine should be collected a short time after it has been passed, in a perfectly clean bottle, holding from four to eight fluidounces. This may be tested at once for reaction, specific gravity, the presence of albumen or sugar, and its color, general appearance, and odor may be noted. In most cases these points may be obtained with sufficient accuracy after twelve hours' and, in the winter, even after twenty-four hours' standing. The urine should then stand ten or twelve hours, to allow of the deposition of a sediment, the general appearance of which should also be noted. It may remain in the original bottle, or the sediment may be allowed to deposit in a conical vessel A, covered with a porcelain plate, on which the memoranda may be written in pencil. In specimens brought by patients, it is as well to have the urine stand in the original bottle,

Fig. 1.

G. TIEMANN CO.

Vessel for collecting urinary deposits.

but the conical glasses are very convenient for specimens freshly collected. In about twelve hours specimens of the sediment should be taken up with a pipette or drop-tube, to be examined microscopically.

The points to be noted in ordinary chemical examinations are the following:

1. The general appearance and color; the time of the day when the specimen was taken; the general appearance of the deposit, if any exist; the total quantity in the twenty-four hours; and the odor.

2. The reaction; whether acid, alkaline, or neutral.

3. The specific gravity.

4. The presence or absence of albumen.

5. The presence or absence of sugar.

6. The presence or absence of biliary matters, in case the color should lead to the suspicion of their existence.

*General Appearance, Color, and Odor.*—I have found it very convenient, in recording urinary examinations, to use pieces of colored paper, gummed on the back, that will represent approximatively the color of the specimen as it appears in the vessel for taking specific gravity. A small piece of the paper is cut off and attached to the record, with the remark, clear or turbid, as the case may be. With regard to the odor, it may be noted as normal, strongly or feebly urinous, sweetish, ammoniacal, fetid, or by some term that will indicate any extraneous odorous principle.

*Reaction.*—The most convenient method of determining the reaction of the urine, is by delicately-tinted blue litmus-paper for acid urine, and faintly-reddened litmus or turmeric paper for alkaline urine. Normal urine is usually acid, and consequently turns blue litmus red. If it be alkaline, it restores the blue color to reddened litmus, and changes yellow turmeric paper brown. It is not usually important to determine the amount of acidity of the urine, but this may be done by neutralizing with alkaline solutions that have been graduated to represent a known quantity of crystallized oxalic acid. It is frequently useful to determine whether the alkalinity of a specimen of urine be due to a fixed alkali (potash or soda), or to a volatile alkali, the result of ammoniacal decomposition. If the urine contain a fixed alkali, the blue color of the litmus will remain after the paper has been thoroughly dried; and if the reaction be due to a volatile alkali, the blue color will disappear from the paper as the moisture evaporates. In the treatment of certain diseases, one of the objects is to keep the urine alkaline; and perhaps the most convenient test to employ constantly, in these cases, is the turmeric paper.

*Specific Gravity.*—The only absolutely accurate way of taking the specific gravity of any liquid is by actual weight of a definite volume; but this requires a delicate balance, carefully adjusted, and the process must occupy considerable time. The most convenient method in ordinary examinations is by floating in the liquid a glass urinometer, when the number of degrees above 1000 may be read off from the scale. (See Fig. 2.) The urinometers in the set of apparatus I am describing may be compared with the standard in the posses-

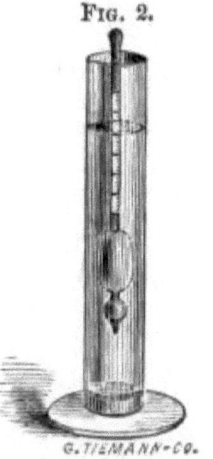

FIG. 2.

G. TIEMANN-CO.

Apparatus for specific gravity.

sion of Messrs. Tiemann & Co., which has been tested by actual weight throughout the entire scale. Of course, the specific gravity varies slightly with temperature. Corrections for temperature may be made from table B. The usual standard for the specific gravity of liquids is 60° Fahr. It may be useful sometimes to form an idea from the specific gravity, of the total amount of solids excreted; and it is a curious fact that between 1010 and 1030, the last two figures indicating the specific gravity indicate also, with a very slight error, the number of grains of solids in the urine per fluidounce. Table C gives the weight of a fluidounce of urine and the proportion of solids when the specific gravity is between 1010 and 1039.

In diabetic urine, the relations of the specific gravity to the proportion of sugar are so variable and uncertain that it is best, in cases in which accurate estimates are desired, to have recourse to quantitative analysis.

*Presence or Absence of Albumen.*—There are two tests which, if used together, will easily and certainly determine the presence or absence of albumen in urine, and these are heat and nitric acid.

If a specimen of albuminous urine of a decidedly acid reaction be boiled, it will become more or less turbid or opaque, in proportion to the quantity of albumen that is present. A method very generally recommended is to fill a test-tube about half-full of urine and apply the heat to the upper layer, which, if it be rendered turbid, will present a marked contrast with the clear fluid below. If the urine be neutral or alkaline, a few drops of acetic acid should be added before the heat is applied. In urine that is very feebly acid, neutral, or alkaline, turbidity may follow the application of heat when no albumen is present. This is due to a deposition of the earthy phosphates; and the character of this precipitate may be recognized by adding a drop or two of nitric acid, which immediately clears up the specimen. In urine containing a large quantity of albumen, opacity is produced at a comparatively low temperature; but if the proportion of albumen be small, cloudiness may not appear until the liquid has been brought to the boiling-point. In urine that is turbid from urates, heat will first dissolve the precipitate and render the liquid clear; and afterward, as the temperature is raised, the albumen will be coagulated.

In the test by nitric acid the reagent may be simply dropped in, or, as is recommended by some, it may be allowed to trickle along the side of the test-tube and fall to the bottom. In most specimens of albuminous urine, the nitric acid simply added to the urine will produce a well-marked coagulation. When the acid is carefully passed to the bottom of the tube, there is a clear stratum below formed by the acid, a clear stratum of urine above, and an intermediate zone of coagulation, more or less opaque. When the urine contains an excess of urea, the addition of nitric acid sometimes produces a precipitate of nitrate of urea, but this is dissipated by gentle heat.

As a general proposition, it may be stated that urine in which there is an opacity produced by heat that is not cleared up by nitric acid, or in which there is a precipitation by nitric acid that does not disappear with gentle heat, is sure to contain albumen.

*Presence or Absence of Sugar.*—The ordinary methods for detecting sugar in clear solutions, particularly the test with sulphate of copper and caustic potash, cannot be certainly and easily applied to the urine. If the test-liquids be added to the urine and the mixture be boiled, normal urine will decolorize the solution, and it is frequently difficult to form a negative opinion with regard to the presence of sugar. Almost all writers who have had practical experience with these processes have recognized the difficulties in this mode of using the copper-tests; and the various other tests that have been proposed are neither very delicate nor convenient.

In view of these facts, it has been suggested by Roberts and others, that the test-liquid be boiled and the urine added drop by drop; and in this way the detection of sugar becomes as certain and easy as the test for albumen. Roberts uses the preparation known as Fehling's test-liquid, the formula for which, reduced to English grains, is as follows:

Sulphate of copper, 94·73 grains (40 grammes); neutral tartrate of potash, 378·91 grains (160 grammes); solution of caustic soda, specific gravity, 1·12 (about 16½° of Baumé's hydrometer), 3½ fluidounces (750 grammes). Add water to make exactly 6 fluid-ounces (1154·5 cubic centimetres).

If prepared by the English weights, exactly 200 grains of the test-liquid will correspond to one grain of sugar. If prepared by the French weights, ten cubic centimetres correspond to 0·05 of a gramme of sugar.[1]

For merely determining the presence or absence of sugar in any given specimen of urine, an ordinary test-tube is filled to the depth of about an inch with the test-liquid, which is boiled, when the urine is added drop by drop. In ordinary diabetic urine the first few drops will produce a brilliant reddish or yellowish opaque precipitate. If the urine be added to about the volume of the test-liquid and the mixture be again brought to the boiling-point, without any precipitate, it is certain that no sugar is present.

The only practical inconvenience in the use of

[1] ROBERTS, *op. cit.*, p. 147. I have given the French weights in parenthesis, with the proportions the same, though the absolute quantities are different. Through the kindness of Dr. Ryerson, who has carefully revised all of the tables and formulæ of the first edition, I am enabled to make important corrections in the reduction, by Roberts, of the French to the English weights and measures (see preface to the second edition).

this test is in the fact that the liquid is liable to alteration by keeping, and when it is thus altered it will precipitate by simple boiling; but as boiling is a necessary preliminary to the test, there can be no error when the process is followed out with care. If the liquid be imperfect from keeping, all that is necessary, in ordinary examinations, is to add a little more soda and filter; but in all accurate analyses, a fresh preparation should be made. To obviate this inconvenience, however, I have been in the habit of keeping three distinct liquids, and mixing them for use, as follows:

Solution of sulphate of copper 94·73 grains in a fluidounce of distilled water; solution of neutral tartrate of potash, 378·91 grains in an ounce; solution of caustic soda, sp. gr. 1·12, or 16½° Baumé.

Measure half a fluidrachm of the solution of copper, add half a fluidrachm of the solution of tartrate of potash, add fifteen minims of distilled water, and add the solution of soda to make three fluidrachms. In ordinary tests I mix in a test-tube about one part of copper, one part of potash, and four parts of soda, which answers perfectly well. In using this formula for the preparation of a liquid for quantitative analyses, it is particularly important to be accurate with regard to the quantity of the solution of copper and the entire quantity of the mixture, for it is the decomposition of the copper which indicates the amount of sugar.

The only one of these three liquids that is liable to serious decomposition is the solution of neutral tartrate of potash, which may become in part changed into a carbonate and effervesce when mixed with the copper; but this does not affect the test in its ordinary applications.

*Presence or Absence of Bile.*—The presence of the coloring matter of the bile is usually indicated by the characteristic tint, more or less strongly marked, in the urine. A simple and certain test is to spread a thin stratum of the urine upon a porcelain surface, and add to it a drop of nitroso-nitric acid (a mixture of nitrous with nitric acid). If biliverdine be present, the drop of acid will be fringed with a rapidly-varying play of colors, violet, green, and red, which speedily disappear. A drop of nitric acid will produce nearly the same appearance, though the colors are less strongly marked.

It is stated that the biliary acids sometimes appear in the urine, but it does not seem that their characteristic reaction is ever very distinct. The best mode of detecting these principles is by Pettenkoffer's test, which is applied in the following way:

To the suspected fluid add a few drops of a strong solution of cane-sugar. Then add strong

sulphuric acid, drop by drop, to about one-half c
two-thirds the volume of the original liquid.   If th
biliary salts be present in large quantity, a red colc
shows itself almost immediately at the bottom o
the test-tube, and soon extends through the entir
liquid, rapidly deepening until it becomes of a dar
lake or purple.   These changes are very slow i:
the presence of a small quantity of the biliary salt:
and may occupy from fifteen to twenty minute:
These are the phenomena observed in ordinary clea
solutions of the biliary salts.   In the urine the re
action is indefinite and unsatisfactory

Analysis for albumen—Analysis for sugar—Differential-density method of analysis for sugar—Volumetric method for estimating sugar—Quantitative analysis for urea—Quantitative analysis for chlorine, sulphuric acid, phosphoric acid, and uric acid.

IT is frequently very important, in the progress of a case, to be able to ascertain from time to time the amount of urea, urates, or sugar contained in the urine ; and these points may be determined very easily and rapidly by volumetric processes. It is also a very simple problem to determine the proportion of chlorine, sulphuric acid, and phosphoric acid ; but, with regard to the last two, although a great many observations have been made on the urine in health and disease, it has not been ascertained that their variations are connected with any definite pathological conditions. I have omitted, in the list of reagents required in ordinary examinations, the liquids for quantitative

analysis for sulphuric acid, phosphoric acid,
uric acid.  Of course, these acids actually (
in the urine only in combination with bases, b
is usually sufficient to ascertain their propor(
without calculating the amount of the salts.

*Quantitative Analysis for Albumen.*—To a(
tain the proportion of dry albumen, a small q
tity of acetic acid is added to a weighed quan
of urine, and the specimen is boiled in a test-t
The precipitate may then be collected on a fi
carefully dried and weighed, and its proportion
culated.  This estimate, however, is seldom requi

A rough but sufficiently accurate estimate (
be made by adding acetic acid, boiling, and al.
ing the flaky precipitate to settle.  Its propor
may then be expressed as one-eighth, one-fou
etc., as the case may be.

*Quantitative Analysis for Sugar.*—Rob
recommends an exceedingly easy process for q(
titative examinations of sugar, so rapid that it (
be employed from day to day in ordinary case(
diabetes.  This he calls the "differential den
method." [1]  Professor Doremus has made repe(
experiments with this process, and agrees with
Roberts with regard to its accuracy.  The estin

Two specimens of diabetic urine are taken, one for comparison and the other for analysis. To one is added a small lump of German yeast, in a bottle, with a nicked cork, to allow of the escape of gas; and the other specimen is placed in a similar bottle, tightly corked. The two bottles are then set aside in a warm place, as the mantel-piece in winter, or in the sun in summer. In twenty-four hours the fermentation will have been completed in the specimen to which yeast has been added. If the specific gravity of the two be now compared, the fermented specimen will be found much the lighter, from loss of sugar which has been decomposed into alcohol and carbonic acid. The difference in the density of the two specimens, expressed in degrees of the urinometer, will represent the number of grains of sugar per fluidounce in the urine. For example, if the specific gravity of the fermented specimen be 1010, and the specific gravity of the unfermented specimen, 1040, the urine contains 30 grains of sugar per fluidounce. In this process it is essential to compare the densities of the two specimens at the same temperature.

The volumetric method is a little more troublesome, though it is also very simple. Fehling's test-liquid is made up by the formula already given (see p. 37), and 200 grains are measured off in a tube graduated for that purpose. The diabetic urine is then diluted with water, so that the proportion of urine shall be one in five or ten. The test-liquid is diluted

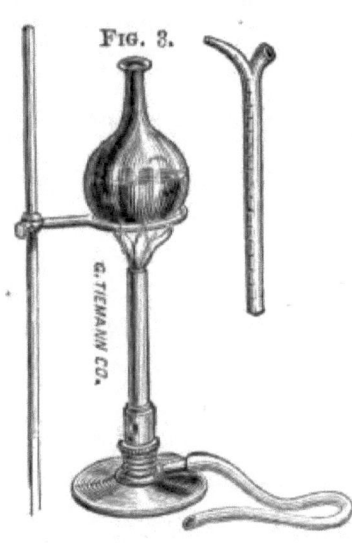

FIG. 3.

Apparatus for volumetric analysis for sugar.

with about twice its volume of water, and placed in a small flask. A graduated burette is now filled with the diluted urine to 0. The test is then boiled over a ring with wire-gauze, and the diluted urine is added in small quantities, producing each time a copious red precipitate, and gradually discharging the blue color. After every addition of urine, the mixture should be brought again to the boiling-point, and a few seconds allowed each time for the precipitate to fall. When the blue color has disappeared, and no further precipitate is formed by adding the urine, the analysis is complete. As the two hundred grains of the test used exactly correspond to one grain of sugar, by reading off the number of grains added from the burette, the calculation may be easily made. For example, if the urine be diluted so that ten parts of the mixture represent one of urine, and if one hundred grains of the mixture be used from the burette, ten grains of urine contain one grain of sugar. This gives the proportion of sugar per hundred or thousand. By reference to table C, which gives the weight of a fluidounce of urine of different specific gravities, the amount of sugar per fluidounce, and afterward the total quantity in the twenty-four hours, may be calculated, by multiplying the weight of a fluidounce by the percentage of sugar, and dividing by 100.[1] To facilitate these estimates, I have calculated a table, which gives the proportion of sugar in the undiluted urine represented by the graduations on the scale, supposing one part of urine to be diluted with nine of water. In urine diluted with four parts of water, the indications are to be doubled.

*Quantitative Analysis for Urea.*—Several ac curate, but at the same time complicated pro-cesses have been devised by chemists for determin-ing the proportion of urea in the urine; but it becomes so often necessary for the physician to be able to measure the daily excretion of urea, particularly in organic diseases of the kidneys, that it is exceedingly desirable to fix upon some

---

[1] Inasmuch as the grains of the diluted urine are represented in the burette by volume, and not by actual weight, there is neces-sarily a slight error in the calculation, depending upon differences in the specific gravity of the specimens; but, in urine so much diluted, this error is unimportant, and may practically be disregarded.

method, sufficiently accurate for practical pur
but so rapid and easy that it may be employed
stantly by the busy practitioner. Liebig's
metric method is the one most frequently emp
by chemists, but this is somewhat complicated
is liable to some sources of error. Bunsen's me
is perhaps more generally applicable to all c
tions of the urine, but it is difficult. By fa
simplest process is known as Davy's method,
the hypochlorite of soda, or Labarraque's solu
The only question is with regard to its accu
In describing this process, Dr. Davy states th
has repeatedly compared it with Liebig's me
and has found it to correspond so nearly tha
slight difference could be disregarded. I hav
rived at this conclusion in the same way, usin
imported French Labarraque's solution, but
found the test very uncertain with the Ame
article, in some instances obtaining not more
one-half of the proper quantity of gas. I hav
hesitation in saying that, with the French solu
the method is all that could ever be desired b
medical practitioner. In describing this proce
cannot do better than to quote the directions g
by Thudichum : [1]

[1] THUDICHUM, *A Treatise on the Pathology of the Urine.*
don, 1858, p. 69.

"A strong glass tube, about twelve or fourteen inches long, closed at one end, and its open extremity ground smooth, and having the bore not larger than the thumb conveniently can cover, holding from two to three cubic inches, each divided into tenths and hundredths by graduation on the glass, is filled more than a third full of mercury, to which afterward a measured quantity of urine to be examined is poured, which may be from a quarter of a drachm to a drachm or upward, according to the capacity of the tube ; then holding the tube in one hand near its open extremity, and having the thumb in readiness to cover the aperture, the operator fills it completely full with a solution of the hypochlorite of soda (taking care not to overflow the tube), and then instantly covers the opening tightly with the thumb, and having rapidly inverted the tube once or twice, to mix the urine with the hypochlorite, he finally opens the tube under a saturated solution of common salt in water, contained in a steady cup or small mortar. The mercury then flows out, and the solution of salt takes its place, and the mixture of urine and hypochlorite being lighter than the solution of salt, will remain in the upper part of the tube, and will therefore be prevented from descending and mixing with the fluid in the cup. A rapid disengagement of minute globules of gas soon takes place in the mixture in the upper part of the tube, and the gas is there retained and collected. The tube is then left in the upright position till there is no further appearance of minute globules of gas being formed, the time being dependent upon the strength of the hypochlorite and the quantity of urea present; but the decomposition is generally completed in from three to four hours; it may, however, be left much longer, even for a day if convenient, and having set the experiment going, it requires no further attention; and when the decomposition is completed, it is only necessary to read the quantity of gas produced off the scale on the tube. In cases where great accuracy is required, due attention must be paid to the temperature and atmospheric pressure, and certain corrections made if these deviate from the usual standards of comparison, at the time of reading off the volume of the gas; but in most cases sufficiently near approximations to accuracy may be obtained without reference to those particulars."

I have been in the habit of following the above process exactly, using for the estimate half a fluidrachm of urine. Each cubic inch of gas represents 0·645 of a grain of urea. To obtain the proportion, multiply the fractions of a cubic inch graduated on the tube by 0·645, and the result will be the amount of urea in half a fluidrachm, in grains. Multiply by sixteen to obtain the proportion per fluidounce, or the entire quantity in the twenty-four hours may be calculated, if a specimen of the mixed urine of the twenty-four hours have been used. By reference to table C, the weight of a fluidounce with the specific gravity may be taken, and from this may be calculated the proportion of urea per 1,000 parts. The apparatus used in this analysis is represented in Fig. 4.

To further facilitate the estimate of the proportion of urea, I have calculated table E, which gives the number of grains of urea per fluidounce represented by the divisions of the scale on the tube graduated in cubic inches. This is calculated, supposing that half a fluidrachm of urine has been used. To calculate the percentage of urea, refer to table C, for the weight of a fluidounce of urine in propor-

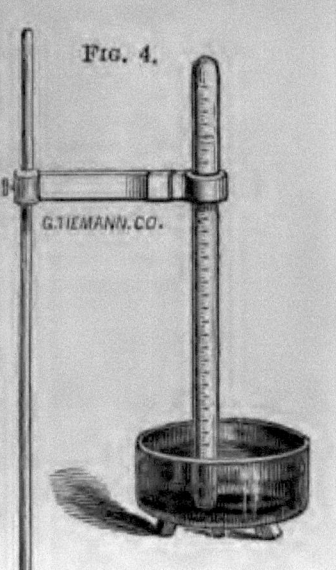

FIG. 4.

G.TIEMANN.CO.

Apparatus for determining the proportion of urea in the urine.

tion to its specific gravity. Multiply the grains of urea per fluidounce by 100, and divide by the weight of a fluidounce of the specimen.

*Quantitative Analysis for Chlorine, Sulph*
*Acid, and Phosphoric Acid.*—It is not so ofter
portant to the physician to ascertain the pro
tions in the urine of the principles above enu
ated, as to estimate the amount of urea or su;
but by the volumetric method there is little
culty in making quantitative estimates of chlor
sulphuric acid, and phosphoric acid. Beyond
however, in the present condition of medical
ence, there is little important information to
obtained from chemical examination of the u
so imperfectly do we understand the physiolog
and pathological relations of the other normal
abnormal ingredients of this excretion.

I am indebted to my colleague, Dr. R. O. L
mus, Professor of Chemistry in the Bellevue I
pital Medical College, and his assistant, Dr. A.
Wilkinson, for valuable assistance in preparing
formulæ of the following test-liquids, for chlor
phosphoric and sulphuric acid, in solutions, gr
ated so that each fluidounce will correspond to
grains of the principle to be estimated in the ur
Prof. Doremus appreciates fully the great im
tance to the practical physician of simple and
tests; and the want of absolute accuracy w
some of these methods present is so slight that it
practically be disregarded, in view of the cons

and unimportant variations in the urine in health and disease. Each one of these solutions represents in half a fluidounce one grain of the substance sought for, and half a fluidounce will fall a little short of filling the burette, graduated to two hundred and fifty grains. To make the tests still more delicate, without complicating the process, I propose to use the burette. Into this is poured a carefully-measured half-ounce of the test-liquid, the burette being then filled to 0 with distilled water. Every division of the burette into two grains will then represent $\frac{2}{250}$ of a grain. Always using the same quantity of urine (two fluidrachms), I have calculated a table in which the proportion per fluidounce for either chlorine, sulphuric acid, or phosphoric acid, is given opposite the number of the divisions on the burette.

*Chlorine.*—In a fluid so complex in its composition as the urine, it is by no means a simple matter to estimate with absolute accuracy the proportion of chlorine; still, as far as any information valuable to the practical physician is concerned, the precipitation of chlorine from an acidulated solution by nitrate of silver is sufficiently exact.

To prepare the test-liquid, make a solution of chemically pure fused nitrate of silver in distilled water, so that six fluidounces shall ᵃᵒⁿ⁻ᵗ grains of the salt. A fluidounce of this solution will correspond to two grains of chlorine.

To estimate the amount of chlorine in a given specimen, measure out carefully two fluidrachms of urine, and add a few drops of nitric acid, to keep the phosphates in solution when the nitrate of silver is added. Measure out now half a fluidounce of the test-liquid, pour it into the burette, and carefully fill with distilled water to 0. The urine may now be diluted with water, if it be desired to make the estimate with great nicety, or the undiluted urine may be used.

The solution is then gradually added to the urine from the burette, each addition being followed by a white precipitate. Each time, after adding the test-liquid, the mixture should be stirred with a glass rod, and the precipitate allowed to settle. At the moment when the addition of the test-liquid fails to produce a precipitate, the analysis is complete. This test will occupy from ten to fifteen minutes.

Each division of the scale on the burette into two grains represents $\frac{2}{250}$ of a grain of chlorine. In table F, I have calculated the proportion per fluidounce of urine, supposing the quantity of urine used to have been two fluidrachms.

If the urine be albuminous, two fluidrachms should be carefully measured, acidulated with a little acetic acid, and boiled.   The coagulated albumen may now be separated by filtration, the clear filtrate acidulated with nitric acid, and then treated with the graduated solution of nitrate of silver.

*Sulphuric Acid.*—The same remark made concerning the accuracy of the preceding test for chlorine is applicable to the process for estimating the sulphuric acid of the urine by a graduated solution of chloride of barium.   For all ordinary purposes, however, the test I am about to describe is sufficiently exact.

The test-liquid is simply a solution of chemically pure chloride of barium, six fluidounces of which contain 36·6 grains of the salt.   A fluidounce of this solution represents exactly two grains of sulphuric acid.

To apply the test, two fluidrachms of urine are measured, as for the other tests, and acidulated with a few drops of nitric acid.   If the urine be albuminous, it may be acidulated with acetic acid, boiled, filtered, and the filtrate treated with nitric acid.

Half a fluidounce of the test-liquid is now poured into the burette, which is filled with distilled water to 0.   The solution is then added from the burette little by little, stirring the mixture with a glass rod, and waiting for the deposit to subside, which takes place more rapidly than in the test for chlorides.

When the addition of a fresh quantity of the solution fails to produce a precipitate, the test is complete.  The amount of the solution that has been
added may then be read off from the burette, every
division of which into two grains represents $\frac{2}{250}$ of
a grain of sulphuric acid.

Supposing the quantity of urine used to have
been two fluidrachms, the proportion of sulphuric
acid per fluidounce is given in table F.

*Phosphoric Acid.*—The process for determining
the proportion of phosphoric acid in the urine is not
open to any serious objection on the score of want
of accuracy, and, after the proper solutions have
been prepared, the estimate may be made rapidly
and presents no difficulty.  I copy the following
theory of this process from the excellent work of
Neubauer and Vogel:[1]

"A solution of phosphate of soda, which contains also both acetate of soda and free acetic acid,
when treated with a dilute solution of perchloride
(sesquichloride) of iron, yields a voluminous whit-
ish-yellow precipitate of phosphate of iron, containing one equivalent of oxide of iron to one equivalent
of phosphoric acid.  So that, if we add acetate of

soda to a solution containing an unknown quantity of phosphoric acid, and then add a standard solution of perchloride of iron until the whole of the phosphoric acid is thrown down, and a trace of the iron appears in the mixture, we can reckon the quantity of phosphoric acid, by taking the amount of iron-solution employed."

This process requires three solutions, viz.; a graduated solution of sesquichloride of iron, a solution of acetate of soda containing free acetic acid, and a solution of ferrocyanide of potassium, the last being used to detect the first trace of an excess of iron. These solutions are prepared as follows:

For the solution of sesquichloride of iron, take 9·33 grains of pure iron (piano-forte wire has been recommended, but iron by hydrogen is better) and dissolve in pure hydrochloric acid, adding a little nitric acid. Evaporate this carefully to dryness in a water-bath, in order to drive off the excess of hydrochloric acid, and dissolve the residue in six fluidounces of distilled water. One fluidounce of this solution will correspond to two grains of phosphoric acid.

For the second solution, dissolve 400 grains of acetate of soda in six fluidounces of water, and add 800 grains of ordinary acetic acid. Half of a fluidrachm of this solution is to be added to two flui-

drachms of urine, before adding the solution of perchloride of iron.

The third solution is simply ferrocyanide of
potassium in water, and the strength is not important. I have prepared it in the proportion of
twelve grains to six fluidounces.

To estimate the entire amount of phosphoric acid
in a given specimen, measure off two fluidrachms
of urine, and add half a fluidrachm of the solution of
acetate of soda and acetic acid. Pour half a fluidounce of the solution of sesquichloride of iron into
the burette, and dilute with distilled water to 0. The
iron-solution is now to be gradually added to the mixture of urine, this producing a yellowish precipitate.
During this process, the mixture is stirred with a
glass rod, and a drop is taken from time to time,
put upon a bit of filtering-paper, which is pressed
with the fingers over a second piece of filtering-
paper moistened with the solution of ferrocyanide
of potassium. The faintest blue color appearing on
the paper moistened with the solution of ferrocyanide of potassium is an indication that an excess
of iron is present in the mixture, and the analysis
is then complete. The amount of iron-solution
added may then be read off from the burette, and
each division into two grains represents $\frac{2}{50}$ of a
grain of phosphoric acid. The proportion of phos-

phoric acid per fluidounce may then be taken from table F.

To estimate the relative proportions of phosphoric acid combined with alkalies and that combined with earths, the following simple method may be employed:

Measure off two fluidrachms of urine, as before, and add a few drops of ammonia. This will precipitate the earthy phosphates, which after a few hours will deposit, and may be separated by filtration. The filtrate is collected, and the residue on the filter is washed with water, containing a little ammonia, which is also collected. The liquid, containing in solution the phosphoric acid combined with alkalies, is now carefully neutralized with acetic acid, and treated with the acetate-of-soda solution and the iron-solution in the manner just described. By this means the amount of phosphoric acid combined with alkalies is estimated, and this, subtracted from the entire amount of phosphoric acid in the urine, will give the proportion of phosphoric acid combined with earths.

*Quantitative Analysis for Uric Acid.*—After a thorough trial of the only volumetric method for the determination of the uric acid in the urine that has been recommended as at all accurate, it became evident that its process was so uncertain as to be entirely unavailable in clinical examinations. I was compelled, therefore, to have recourse to the more tedious process of estimating the acid by weight. The process which I finally adopted is easy enough, but requires care and the use of a balance. Its theory is briefly as follows :

Absolute alcohol, added to urine evaporated to a syrup, will dissolve urea, creatine, creatinine, and coloring matter, leaving the urates and the inorganic salts. By washing the residue of an alcoholic extract with dilute hydrochloric acid, the inorganic salts are removed, leaving the uric acid set free from its combinations, which may be collected and weighed. The following are the manipulations to be employed in this analysis :

Take one fluidounce of urine, filtered, so as to remove any mucus that it may contain. The urine is then evaporated over a water-bath, to the consistence of a thick syrup, in a porcelain evaporating-dish. To hasten the evaporation, the liquid is spread over the sides of the dish with a glass rod from time to time, as the evaporation is approaching completion. When it is so thick as to adhere to the vessel, add about half a fluidounce of absolute alcohol, mixing the urine with the alcohol thoroughly, and pouring it upon a filter which has been previously weighed dry, and then moistened with alcohol. Extract in this way with alcohol two or three times, or until the alcohol no longer takes up any coloring matter.

After pouring off the alcohol upon the filter, the residue left in the evaporating-dish should be extracted in the same way with a mixture of one part of hydrochloric acid to six of water, and the whole poured on the filter used to separate the alcoholic extract. In this part of the process, about a fluidounce of the acid solution should be used. The residue on the filter should then be washed with a wash-bottle, two or three times with the acid, and afterward with distilled water.

After the liquid has separated, the filter is dried in a water-oven and carefully weighed. The increase in weight (the filter having been previously weighed), represents the amount of uric acid per fluidounce of urine.

The process of evaporating will be much hastened by stirring the urine. A glass rod with a small piece of rubber-tubing attached to the end is very convenient for cleaning the residue from the evaporating-dish, but the rubber should be carefully washed, so that no particles can be lost. The lip of the evaporating dish may be smeared at its lower edge with a little grease, to prevent any loss of fluid in pouring.

If there be any crystals of uric acid in the specimen, these may be collected on the filter before evaporating.

For the minute details of this process, I am indebted to my assistant, Mr. J. W. S. Arnold. Employed in this way, it presents every element of accuracy that could be desired. Using an ounce of urine, the analysis will occupy little more than an hour.

The only tedious detail in this manipulation is the weighing of the filters. The Swedish filtering paper is the best, and the filter should be moistened with alcohol, and carefully dried in the water-oven until it has ceased to lose weight, before it is used to separate the extracts. In drying the filter, both before and after collecting the uric acid, it should be weighed repeatedly, and the weighing continued until the weight becomes stationary, as this is the only way to determine that the moisture has been entirely removed.

# APPENDIX.

THE examination of urinary concretions is so very simple and requires so little apparatus, that I am led to describe briefly, in this connection, the methods that will answer all practical purposes in the great majority of instances.

The varieties of calculi usually described are the following: uric acid, urates, oxalate of lime, secondary or fusible phosphates, cystine, xanthine, urostealith, basic phosphate of lime, and carbonate of lime. There are only three varieties, however, the uric acid, oxalate of lime, and phosphatic (fusible), that are at all common; and the others are so rare that they may almost be disregarded. The tests for the common varieties do not present the slightest difficulty.

*Uric-acid Calculi and Gravel.*—This variety constitutes by far the largest proportion of the urinary concretions. The calculi are very variable in size. They usually have a tuberculated surface, and are of a yellowish or reddish color, presenting, in short, all the great variety of shades observed in deposits of the amorphous urates. Uric-acid gravel is also common. The character of these concretions may be readily recognized by the following test:

A small portion of the calculus or gravel is placed upon a glass slide or a porcelain surface, and is covered with a few drops of nitric acid. Under the gentle heat of a spirit-lamp or a gas-flame, it readily dissolves with effervescence and is reduced to a dry residue. After the residue has become cold, a drop of ammonia added will produce a bright-violet color. This is called the murexid test, and it is certain and unmistakable. By this test *laminæ* of uric acid may often be detected in calculi composed of layers of different substances.

*Oxalate-of-lime Calculi and Gravel.*—Calculi of oxalate of lime are quite common, but the gravel is somewhat rare. This is sometimes called the mulberry calculus. The surface is usually tuberculated, though it may be smooth. The color is dark brown or grayish. The calculus is soluble in hydrochloric and in nitric acid. The following is the most convenient test for this variety of concre-

A small portion is heated under a blow-pipe upon a bit of charcoal, or in a small platinum spoon, and it finally burns down to a white ash of caustic lime, the oxalic acid being destroyed. If a portion of this ash be placed upon ·moist, reddened litmus-paper, it instantly strikes an intense blue. This behavior is entirely characteristic of oxalate of lime.

*Calculi of the Mixed Phosphates (fusible Calculi).*—The mixed phosphates, composed of the phosphate of lime and the ammonio-magnesian phosphate, frequently encrust calculi formed either of uric acid or the oxalate of lime. They sometimes form entire calculi of great size. They are friable, often present brilliant crystals of the triple phosphate on their surface, and are very soluble in acids, but insoluble in alkalies. When strongly heated under the blow-pipe, they fuse into a hard enamel. Small quantities of the mixed phosphates very often enter into the composition of calculi composed chiefly of other substances.

With these few directions, the character of any of the ordinary calculi may be readily ascertained, as well as the nature of the nucleus or of the different layers.

## *Care of Apparatus.*

A physician in full practice has frequent occasion to use his apparatus for urinary examinations, and it is essential that it should be always clean and in order. None of the bottles should be allowed to remain empty, for it is impossible to say when the reagents may be most urgently required. When the test-tubes or other glass or porcelain ware have been used, they should be cleaned without delay. To facilitate this, I have provided in the set of apparatus, brushes, swabs, etc., by which these articles can be quickly and efficiently cleaned. Very often the glass becomes stained and clouded by matters that are not readily removed by simple water, and this occurs particularly in the urea-tube. A few drops of sulphuric acid will usually remove any thing of this kind. After using the apparatus for estimating urea, it may be difficult to clean and separate the mercury, but this can be easily done in the following simple way: Pour off the fluid from the mercury, wash it a little with pure water, and then pour it, with the water which cannot easily be separated in the original vessel, into a small funnel closed at the bottom with the finger. The mercury, of course, will occupy the bottom of the funnel, and the water will float upon the top. By partially removing the finger, the mercury may be allowed to escape into a clean vessel, and the funnel is closed again so as to separate the water. The clean mercury is then poured back into its bottle.

FIG. 5.

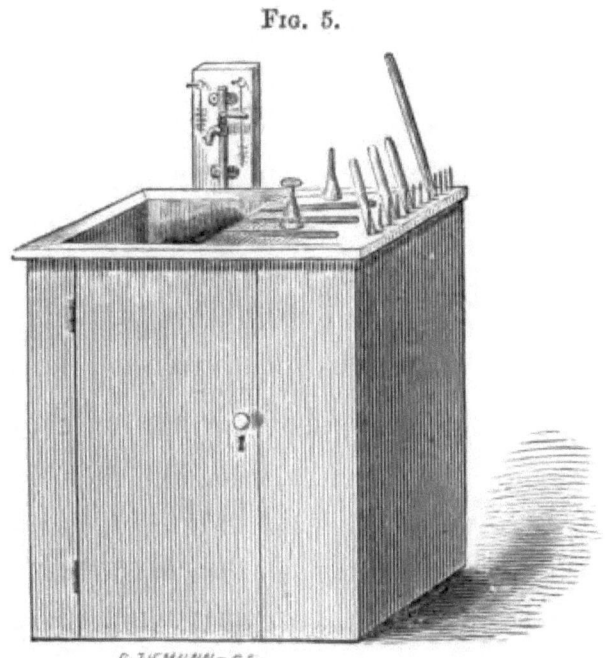

G. TIEMANN & CC.

Sink for cleansing apparatus.

I have had constructed a very convenient little sink about 18 by 24 inches, for cleansing apparatus, of which I give a figure. One half of the top is a simple sink lined with lead, and the other is a grooved board for draining glasses, with a few wooden pins at the end for test-tubes, etc.

## TABLES.

Although the calculations required for determining the proportions of the most important of the urinary constituents by the volumetric method are quite simple, they can be rendered so easy by proper tables, that quantitative analysis seems to be shorn of every difficulty. In preparing and selecting the following tables I have taken those which I have had occasion to use in urinary examinations, and have calculated others, so as to reduce every estimate that is to be made to a tabular form.

*Table A* gives the normal constitution and variations of the human urine. This is taken from the third volume of my work on Physiology. I have added to it an estimate of the normal proportions and variations of urea, chlorine, sulphuric acid, phosphoric acid, and uric acid, per fluidounce, for the reason that the processes recommended for the quantitative determination of these principles give the proportions per fluidounce of urine.

*Table B* gives the corrections to be made for temperature in taking the specific gravity of the urine with a glass urinometer. This is taken from the excellent work on the urine by Golding Bird.

*Table C* gives the number of grains of solids, and the weight of a fluidounce of urine of different densities, from 1001 to 1042. This table, taken in part from Golding Bird, and adapted to the wine-measure, is useful in reducing the proportions of principles per fluidounce to the percentage, and *vice versa.*

*Table D* I have calculated to show the percentage of sugar indicated by the degrees graduated upon the burette used in volumetric analysis.

*Table E* I have calculated to show the number of grains of urea per fluidounce of urine indicated by the degrees on the tube used in the volumetric analysis for this principle.

*Table F* is a general table which I have calculated to show the number of grains per fluidounce of urine, of chlorine, sulphuric acid, or phosphoric acid, indicated by the degrees graduated on the burette used in volumetric analysis. Each one of the liquids used in estimating the principles above enumerated represents one grain of the substance sought for, in half a fluidounce of the test. This uniformity in the graduation of the test-liquids allows the same table to be used for all the estimates.

# A.

## Properties and Composition of the Normal Urine.

Total quantity in 24 hours, 27 to 50 fluidounces. Ordinary range of specific gravity, from 1015 to 1025. Extreme
range of specific gravity, 1005 to 1030. Reaction acid.

### Table of Composition.

| | | |
|---|---|---|
| Water...................................................... | 967·47 to | 940·86 |
| Urea (in 24 hours, 355 to 463 grains—Robin)................. | 15·00 " | 23·00 |
| Urate of soda, neutral and acid.......... ⎫ (In 24 hrs., 6 to | | |
| Urate of ammonia, neutral and acid (in ⎪ 9 grs. of uric acid | | |
|   small quantity)........................ ⎬ —Becquerel—or 9 | | |
| Urate of potassa (traces)................ ⎪ to 14 grs.of urates, | 1·00 " | 1·60 |
| Urate of lime (traces)................... ⎪ estimated as neut. | | |
| Urate of magnesia (traces) .............. ⎭ urate of soda.) | | |
| Hippurate of soda.... ⎫ (In 24 hrs., about 7·5 grs. of hip- | | |
| Hippurate of potassa. ⎬ puric acid—Thudichum—equiv. to | 1·00 " | 1·40 |
| Hippurate of lime.... ⎭ about 8·7 grs. of hippurate of soda.) | | |
| Lactate of soda.... ⎫ | | |
| Lactate of potassa. ⎬ (Daily quantity not estimated)....... | 1·50 " | 2·60 |
| Lactate of lime.... ⎭ | | |
| Creatine.................... ⎫ (In 24 hours, about 11·5 grains | | |
| Creatinine................. ⎬ of both—Thudichum) ........ | 1·60 " | 3·00 |
| Oxalate of lime (daily quantity not estimated)............... | traces " | 1·10 |
| Xanthine...................................................... | not estimated. | |
| Margarine, oleine, and other fatty matters .................... | 0·10 to | 0·20 |
| Chloride of sodium (in 24 hours, about 154 grains—Robin).... | 3·00 " | 8·00 |
| Chloride of potassium ....................................... | traces. | |
| Hydrochlorate of ammonia............................ ....... | 1·50 to | 2·20 |
| Sulphate of soda.... ⎫ (In 24 hrs., 23 to 38 grs. of sulphu- | | |
| Sulphate of potassa. ⎪ ric acid—Thudichum. About equal | | |
| Sulphate of lime ⎬ parts of sulphate of soda and sulphate | 3·00 " | 7·00 |
| (traces).......... ⎪ of potassa—Robin—equiv. to from | | |
| ⎭ 22·5 to 37·5 grs. of each.) | | |
| Phosphate of soda, neutral.. ⎫ (Daily quantity not esti- | | |
| Phosphate of soda, acid..... ⎬ mated) ...................... | 2·50 " | 4·30 |
| Phosphate of magnesia (in 24 hrs., 7·7 to 11·8 grs.—Neubauer). | 0·50 " | 1·00 |
| Phosphate of lime, acid... ⎫ (In 24 hrs., 4·7 to 5·7 grs.— | | |
| Phosphate of lime, basic.. ⎬ Neubauer)..................... | 0·20 " | 1·30 |
| Ammonio-magnesian phosphate (daily quantity not estim.).... | 1·50 " | 2·40 |
| ( Daily excretion of phosphoric acid, about 56 grs.—Thudichum.) | | |
| Silicic acid................................................. | 0·03 " | 0·04 |
| Urrosacine............. ⎫ .................................. | 0·10 " | 0·50 |
| Mucus from the bladder. ⎭ | | |
| | 1,000·00 | 1,000·00 |

## Proportion per Fluidounce of certain of the Urinary Constituents.

The estimates given in this part of the table are roughly approximative, and represent the widest variations consistent with normal conditions. The variations, always considerable, are particularly marked as regards the uric acid, the extremes of which are greater in this than in the table of composition given above:

Urea............................................... 6·50 to 10·50 grains.
Chlorine (1·30 to 3·60 grs. of chloride of sodium.) 0·80 " 2·15 "
Sulphuric acid (1·30 to 3·20 grains of sulphates).. 0·66 " 1·62 "
Phosphoric acid (2·10 to 4·00 grs. of phosphates).. 1·17 " 2·25 "
    do.    Combined with alkalies (phosphate
        of soda and phosphate of mag-
        nesia) ...................... 0·78 " 1·40 "
    do.    Combined with earths (phosphate
        of lime and ammonio-mag-
        nesian phosphate) .......... 0·39 " 0·85 "
Uric acid (0·40 to 0·70 grains of urates)......... 0·23 " 0·40 "

## B.

TABLE FOR REDUCING THE INDICATIONS OF A GLASS URINOMETER TO THE STANDARD TEMPERATURE (60° Fahr.), WHEN THE SPECIFIC GRAVITY HAS BEEN TAKEN AT A HIGHER TEMPERATURE. (BIRD, *Urinary Deposits, etc.*, Philadelphia, 1859, p. 70.)

| Temperature. | No. to be added to the Indication. | Temperature. | No. to be added to the Indication. | Temperature. | No. to be added to the Indication. |
|---|---|---|---|---|---|
| 60° | 0·00 | 69° | 0·80 | 78° | 1·70 |
| 61° | 0·08 | 70° | 0·90 | 79° | 1·80 |
| 62° | 0·16 | 71° | 1·00 | 80° | 1·90 |
| 63° | 0·24 | 72° | 1·10 | 81° | 2·00 |
| 64° | 0·32 | 73° | 1·20 | 82° | 2·10 |
| 65° | 0·40 | 74° | 1·30 | 83° | 2·20 |
| 66° | 0·50 | 75° | 1·40 | 84° | 2·30 |
| 67° | 0·60 | 76° | 1·50 | 85° | 2·40 |
| 68° | 0·70 | 77° | 1·60 | | |

# C.

Table showing the Number of Grains of Solids in, an
the weight of, a Fluidounce of Urine, of every Den
sity, from 1001 to 1042.

This table is chiefly useful in reducing the quantities o
various of the urinary constituents from the proportions pe
fluidounce to the proportions per hundred or thousand. Fo
example, if calculations have been made from tables E or I
of the proportion per fluidounce, of urea, chlorine, sulphuri
acid, or phosphoric acid, these may be reduced to the pe:
centage by multiplying the amount per fluidounce by 1C
and dividing by the weight of a fluidounce of the urine. T
reduce the percentage of sugar calculated from table D t
the proportion per fluidounce, multiply the percentage h
the weight of a fluidounce of the urine and divide by 10
The column giving the amount of solids per fluidounce i
proportion to the specific gravity is not very useful, as it giv
no idea of the proportions of the different solid constituent

| Specific Gravity. | Weight of one Fluidounce. | Solids in one Fluidounce. | Specific Gravity. | Weight of one Fluidounce. | Solids in one Fluidounce. |
|---|---|---|---|---|---|
| 1001 | 456·15 | 1·063 | 1022 | 465·72 | 23·873 |
| 1002 | 456·60 | 2·128 | 1023 | 466·17 | 24·982 |
| 1003 | 457·06 | 3·195 | 1024 | 466·63 | 26·094 |
| 1004 | 457·51 | 4·264 | 1025 | 467·08 | 27·207 |
| 1005 | 457·96 | 5·335 | 1026 | 467·54 | 28·324 |
| 1006 | 458·42 | 6·409 | 1027 | 467·99 | 29·441 |
| 1007 | 458·88 | 7·484 | 1028 | 468·45 | 30·562 |
| 1008 | 459·34 | 8·562 | 1029 | 468·91 | 31·684 |
| 1009 | 459·79 | 9·642 | 1030 | 469·36 | 32·808 |
| 1010 | 460·25 | 10·724 | 1031 | 469·82 | 33·935 |
| 1011 | 460·70 | 11·808 | 1032 | 470·27 | 35·063 |
| 1012 | 461·16 | 12·894 | 1033 | 470·73 | 36·194 |
| 1013 | 461·61 | 13·982 | 1034 | 471·18 | 37·327 |
| 1014 | 462·07 | 15·073 | 1035 | 471·64 | 38·462 |
| 1015 | 462·53 | 16·165 | 1036 | 472·09 | 39·599 |
| 1016 | 462·98 | 17·260 | 1037 | 472·55 | 40·739 |
| 1017 | 463·44 | 18·357 | 1038 | 473·00 | 41·879 |
| 1018 | 463·89 | 19·456 | 1039 | 473·46 | 43·023 |
| 1019 | 464·35 | 20·557 | 1040 | 473·92 | 44·169 |
| 1020 | 464·80 | 21·660 | 1041 | 474·37 | 45·317 |
| 1021 | 465·26 | 22·765 | 1042 | 474·83 | 46·467 |

## D.

**TABLE SHOWING THE PERCENTAGE OF SUGAR IN UNDILUTED DIABETIC URINE, REPRESENTED BY THE DEGREES OF THE SCALE ON THE BURETTE GRADUATED IN GRAINS.**

The urine is supposed to be diluted, so that ten parts of the liquid used represent one of urine; and the quantity of Fehling's test-liquid used is two hundred grains, which is decolorized by exactly one grain of sugar. To ascertain the proportion of sugar per fluidounce, multiply the weight of a fluidounce of urine (see Table C) by the percentage of sugar, and divide by 100.

| Degrees of the Burette. | Percentage of Sugar. | Degrees of the Burette. | Percentage of Sugar. | Degrees of the Burette. | Percentage of Sugar. |
|---|---|---|---|---|---|
| 50 | 20·00 | 118 | 8·47 | 186 | 5·37 |
| 52 | 19·23 | 120 | 8·33 | 188 | 5·32 |
| 54 | 18·52 | 122 | 8·19 | 190 | 5·26 |
| 56 | 17·85 | 124 | 8·06 | 192 | 5·21 |
| 58 | 17·24 | 126 | 7·93 | 194 | 5·15 |
| 60 | 16·66 | 128 | 7·81 | 196 | 5·10 |
| 62 | 16·13 | 130 | 7·69 | 198 | 5·05 |
| 64 | 15·62 | 132 | 7·57 | 200 | 5·00 |
| 66 | 15·15 | 134 | 7·46 | 202 | 4·95 |
| 68 | 14·70 | 136 | 7·35 | 204 | 4·90 |
| 70 | 14·28 | 138 | 7·24 | 206 | 4·85 |
| 72 | 13·80 | 140 | 7·14 | 208 | 4·80 |
| 74 | 13·51 | 142 | 7·04 | 210 | 4·76 |
| 76 | 13·15 | 144 | 6·94 | 212 | 4·72 |
| 78 | 12·82 | 146 | 6·85 | 214 | 4·67 |
| 80 | 12·50 | 148 | 6·76 | 216 | 4·63 |
| 82 | 12·19 | 150 | 6·67 | 218 | 4·59 |
| 84 | 11·90 | 152 | 6·58 | 220 | 4·55 |
| 86 | 11·62 | 154 | 6·49 | 222 | 4·50 |
| 88 | 11·36 | 156 | 6·41 | 224 | 4·46 |
| 90 | 11·11 | 158 | 6·33 | 226 | 4·42 |
| 92 | 10·87 | 160 | 6·25 | 228 | 4·39 |
| 94 | 10·63 | 162 | 6·17 | 230 | 4·35 |
| 96 | 10·41 | 164 | 6·10 | 232 | 4·31 |
| 98 | 10·20 | 166 | 6·03 | 234 | 4·27 |
| 100 | 10·00 | 168 | 5·95 | 236 | 4·23 |
| 102 | 9·80 | 170 | 5·88 | 238 | 4·20 |
| 104 | 9·69 | 172 | 5·81 | 240 | 4·17 |
| 106 | 9·43 | 174 | 5·75 | 242 | 4·13 |
| 108 | 9·26 | 176 | 5·68 | 244 | 4·10 |
| 110 | 9·09 | 178 | 5·62 | 246 | 4·06 |
| 112 | 8·93 | 180 | 5·55 | 248 | 4·03 |
| 114 | 8·77 | 182 | 5·49 | 250 | 4·00 |
| 116 | 8·62 | 184 | 5·43 | | |

4

## E.

TABLE SHOWING THE QUANTITY OF UREA PER FLUIDOUNCE OF
URINE, IN GRAINS, REPRESENTED BY THE DIVISIONS OF THE
SCALE UPON THE TUBE GRADUATED IN CUBIC INCHES.

The tube is filled a little more than one-third full of mercury, upon which is poured half a fluidrachm of urine, and the tube is then filled with solution of hypochlorite of soda, and inverted in a saturated solution of salt in water. To ascertain the percentage of urea, multiply the grains of urea in an ounce by 100, and divide by the weight of a fluidounce of the specimen, taken from Table C. The correction for temperature may be made by adding one per cent. of the volume of gas for every five degrees below 60°, and subtracting the same for every five degrees above 60°.

| Divisions of a Cubic Inch. | Grains of Urea per Fluidounce. | Divisions of a Cubic Inch. | Grains of Urea per Fluidounce. | Divisions of a Cubic Inch. | Grains of Urea per Fluidounce. |
|---|---|---|---|---|---|
| 0·10 | 1·032 | 0·74 | 7·637 | 1·38 | 14·241 |
| 0·12 | 1·238 | 0·76 | 7·843 | 1·40 | 14·448 |
| 0·14 | 1·444 | 0·78 | 8·049 | 1·42 | 14·654 |
| 0·16 | 1·651 | 0·80 | 8·256 | 1·44 | 14·860 |
| 0·18 | 1·857 | 0·82 | 8·462 | 1·46 | 15·067 |
| 0·20 | 2·064 | 0·84 | 8·669 | 1·48 | 15·273 |
| 0·22 | 2·270 | 0·86 | 8·875 | 1·50 | 15·480 |
| 0·24 | 2·476 | 0·88 | 9·081 | 1·52 | 15·686 |
| 0·26 | 2·683 | 0·90 | 9·288 | 1·54 | 15·893 |
| 0·28 | 2·889 | 0·92 | 9·494 | 1·56 | 16·099 |
| 0·30 | 3·096 | 0·94 | 9·701 | 1·58 | 16·305 |
| 0·32 | 3·302 | 0·96 | 9·907 | 1·60 | 16·512 |
| 0·34 | 3·508 | 0·98 | 10·113 | 1·62 | 16·718 |
| 0·36 | 3·715 | 1·00 | 10·320 | 1·64 | 16·925 |
| 0·38 | 3·921 | 1·02 | 10·526 | 1·66 | 17·131 |
| 0·40 | 4·128 | 1·04 | 10·733 | 1·68 | 17·337 |
| 0·42 | 4·334 | 1·06 | 10·939 | 1·70 | 17·544 |
| 0·44 | 4·540 | 1·08 | 11·145 | 1·72 | 17·750 |
| 0·46 | 4·747 | 1·10 | 11·352 | 1·74 | 17·957 |
| 0·48 | 4·953 | 1·12 | 11·558 | 1·76 | 18·163 |
| 0·50 | 5·160 | 1·14 | 11·764 | 1·78 | 18·369 |
| 0·52 | 5·336 | 1·16 | 11·971 | 1·80 | 18·576 |
| 0·54 | 5·573 | 1·18 | 12·177 | 1·82 | 18·782 |
| 0·56 | 5·779 | 1·20 | 12·384 | 1·84 | 18·989 |
| 0·58 | 5·985 | 1·22 | 12·590 | 1·86 | 19·195 |
| 0·60 | 6·192 | 1·24 | 12·796 | 1·88 | 19·401 |
| 0·62 | 6·398 | 1·26 | 13·003 | 1·90 | 19·608 |
| 0·64 | 6·605 | 1·28 | 13·209 | 1·92 | 19·814 |
| 0·66 | 6·811 | 1·30 | 13·416 | 1·94 | 20·021 |
| 0·68 | 7·017 | 1·32 | 13·622 | 1·96 | 20·227 |
| 0·70 | 7·224 | 1·34 | 13·828 | 1·98 | 20·433 |
| 0·72 | 7·430 | 1·36 | 14·035 | 2·00 | 20·640 |

## F.

TABLE SHOWING THE QUANTITY EITHER OF CHLORINE, SUL-
PHURIC ACID, OR PHOSPHORIC ACID, PER FLUIDOUNCE
OF URINE, IN GRAINS, REPRESENTED BY THE DEGREES
OF THE SCALE ON THE BURETTE GRADUATED IN GRAINS.

This table will answer for any of the above-mentioned principles by using one or another of the test-liquids. It is calculated on the supposition that the quantity of urine used is two fluidrachms. To ascertain the percentage, multiply the number of grains per fluidounce by 100, and divide by the weight of a fluidounce of the specimen, taken from table C.

| Degrees of the Burette. | Grains per Fluidounce. | Degrees of the Burette. | Grains per Fluidounce. | Degrees of the Burette. | Grains per Fluidounce. |
|---|---|---|---|---|---|
| 2 | 0·032 | 86 | 1·376 | 170 | 2·720 |
| 4 | 0·064 | 88 | 1·408 | 172 | 2·752 |
| 6 | 0·096 | 90 | 1·440 | 174 | 2·784 |
| 8 | 0·128 | 92 | 1·472 | 176 | 2·816 |
| 10 | 0·160 | 94 | 1·504 | 178 | 2·848 |
| 12 | 0·192 | 96 | 1·536 | 180 | 2·880 |
| 14 | 0·224 | 98 | 1·568 | 182 | 2·912 |
| 16 | 0·256 | 100 | 1·600 | 184 | 2·944 |
| 18 | 0·288 | 102 | 1·632 | 186 | 2·976 |
| 20 | 0·320 | 104 | 1·664 | 188 | 3·008 |
| 22 | 0·352 | 106 | 1·696 | 190 | 3·040 |
| 24 | 0·384 | 108 | 1·728 | 192 | 3·072 |
| 26 | 0·416 | 110 | 1·760 | 194 | 3·104 |
| 28 | 0·448 | 112 | 1·792 | 196 | 3·136 |
| 30 | 0·480 | 114 | 1·824 | 198 | 3·168 |
| 32 | 0·512 | 116 | 1·856 | 200 | 3·200 |
| 34 | 0·544 | 118 | 1·888 | 202 | 3·232 |
| 36 | 0·576 | 120 | 1·920 | 204 | 3·264 |
| 38 | 0·608 | 122 | 1·952 | 206 | 3·296 |
| 40 | 0·640 | 124 | 1·984 | 208 | 3·328 |
| 42 | 0·672 | 126 | 2·016 | 210 | 3·360 |
| 44 | 0·704 | 128 | 2·048 | 212 | 3·392 |
| 46 | 0·736 | 130 | 2·080 | 214 | 3·424 |
| 48 | 0·768 | 132 | 2·112 | 216 | 3·456 |
| 50 | 0·800 | 134 | 2·144 | 218 | 3·488 |
| 52 | 0·832 | 136 | 2·176 | 220 | 3·520 |
| 54 | 0·864 | 138 | 2·208 | 222 | 3·552 |
| 56 | 0·896 | 140 | 2·240 | 224 | 3·584 |
| 58 | 0·928 | 142 | 2·272 | 226 | 3·616 |
| 60 | 0·960 | 144 | 2·304 | 228 | 3·648 |
| 62 | 0·992 | 146 | 2·336 | 230 | 3·680 |
| 64 | 1·024 | 148 | 2·368 | 232 | 3·712 |
| 66 | 1·056 | 150 | 2·400 | 234 | 3·744 |
| 68 | 1·088 | 152 | 2·432 | 236 | 3·776 |
| 70 | 1·120 | 154 | 2·464 | 238 | 3·808 |
| 72 | 1·152 | 156 | 2·496 | 240 | 3·840 |
| 74 | 1·184 | 158 | 2·528 | 242 | 3·872 |
| 76 | 1·216 | 160 | 2·560 | 244 | 3·904 |
| 78 | 1·248 | 162 | 2·592 | 246 | 3·936 |
| 80 | 1·280 | 164 | 2·624 | 248 | 3·963 |
| 82 | 1·312 | 166 | 2·656 | 250 | 4·000 |
| 84 | 1·344 | 168 | 2·688 | | |

FORM FOR RECORDING URINARY EXAMINATIONS (TO BE PRINT
ON A FULL LETTER-SHEET).

## EXAMINATION OF URINE.

*For* ................................................ *at the request* (

*Dr.* ................................................

### PHYSICAL AND CHEMICAL CHARACTERS.

*Total quantity in twenty-four hours,*

*Color,*

*Odor,*

*Reaction,*

*Specific Gravity,*

*Albumen,*

*Sugar,*

*Quantity and General Appearance of the Deposit,*

### MICROSCOPICAL APPEARANCES.

## QUANTITATIVE EXAMINATION.

*Urea, proportion of, per fluidounce,*

  *do.   percentage of,*

  *do.   total quantity of, in twenty-four hours,*

*Chlorine, proportion of, per fluidounce,*

      *do.     percentage of,*

      *do.     total quantity of, in twenty-four hours,*

*Sulphuric Acid, proportion of, per fluidounce,*

          *do.       percentage of,*

          *do.       total quantity of, in twenty-four hours,*

*Phosphoric Acid, proportion of, per fluidounce,*

          *do.       percentage of,*

          *do.       total quantity of, in twenty-four hours,*

          *do.       proportion of, combined with alkalies,*

          *do.       proportion of, combined with earths,*

*Uric Acid, proportion of, per fluidounce,*

      *do.    percentage of,*

      *do.    total quantity of, in twenty-four hours,*